M.A.D.L.Y.®
Mom And Dad Love You

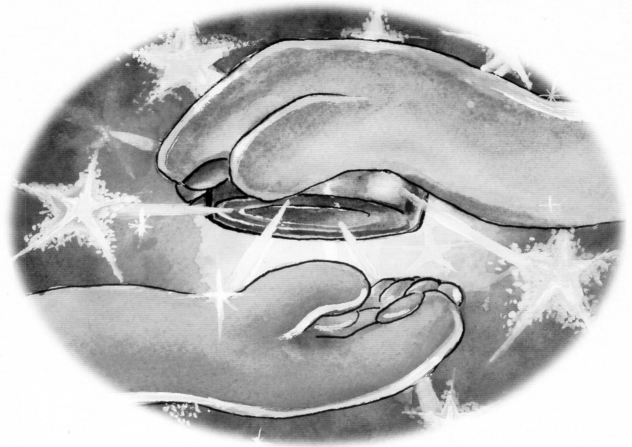

story by
Sally North

illustrated by
Melissa Weisman

Colorbök
Dexter, Michigan

A special thanks to my mom and dad - for all the years of constant love and support they have given me.
-M.W.

Thanks to Jack Morrow for inspiring this book and for all his hard work.
-S.N.

Thanks to all of our family and friends for their support and encouragement.
-S.N.

This book is dedicated to my son, Michael, who taught me how much children need to know that they are loved. Saying it isn't enough - you have to show it everyday.
-S.N.

First U.S. edition 2000

ISBN 1-58508-240-6

10 9 8 7 6 5 4 3 2 1

Printed in Hong Kong

The pictures in this book were done in Watercolor, Gouache, and Ink.

Colorbök
2716 Baker Road
Dexter, MI 48130

This very special story
was given to

_____

MADLY

This is a story
about Bobby the bear.
He lived in a forest,
with trees everywhere.
He played until sundown
with Georgia the goose.
His other best friend
was Marcel the moose.

There were hundreds of fun things
to do in the woods.
Bobby loved to play baseball.
He really was good!
They also played soccer.
They loved hide and seek.
And most afternoons,
they would swim
in the creek.

He had a nice family,
one sister, one brother,
a dad who was funny,
a wonderful mother!
They did lots of fun things
when he was a cub,
and he always had fun
with his toys in the tub.

When Bobby got older,
he started in school.
He carried a backpack.
He thought he was cool!

He missed all the playing,
but school was fun, too.
He learned how to read
and to add two plus two.

When Bobby came home after school everyday,
his mom was there waiting, and here's what she'd say:
"Did you have a good day?
Did you learn something new?
Do you have any homework?
Do you know I love you!"

Then he'd have a snack,
and he'd fly out the door.
    He played with his friends,
    and they never got bored.

They played soccer or baseball
or went for a swim.
Or played hide and seek
until time to go in.

Then the next day,
he started all over again.
He headed for school
with his two favorite friends.
He learned about English
and science and math.
He learned to draw objects
and numbers and graphs.

And when he came home after school every day,
his mom was there waiting, and here's what she'd say:
"Did you have a good day?
Did you learn something new?
Do you have any homework?
Do you know I love you!"

The years went by quickly, and Bobby did well.
He learned how to multiply, study and spell.
He brought home his report cards to show mom and dad.
He always felt proud of the good grades that he had.

He just couldn't show them.
He felt too afraid.
So he hid his report card
from his mom and his dad,
so they wouldn't know
of the bad grade that he had.

But soon his mom found it
right under his bed!

When he came home from school,
here's just what she said:
"Did you have a good day?
Did you learn something new?
Do you have any homework?
Do you know I love you!"

Bobby thought, "They still love me,
even though I did bad.
I just should have told them
about the grade that I had."

"Now about this report card...I found here today.
Why didn't you show us?
What have you to say?"

"I want you to love me,
so I was afraid
to show my report card
that had a bad grade."

She reached in her pocket and took Bobby's hand.
Then she placed something in it,
so shiny and grand.
A coin with one word on it,
"M.A.D.L.Y." it read.

He looked at his mother,
and here's what she said:

"When you have a poor day, or your friends treat you bad;
if you have lots of homework, or feel kind of sad;
wherever you are, and whatever you do...
Remember, M.A.D.L.Y. means

'Mom And Dad Love You!'"

So now when he's playing
or while he's at school,

when he's running

or swimming

or thinking he's cool,

he can reach in his pocket,
and it's always there;
the coin that reminds him
that mom and dad care.

He smiles to himself as he lies down in bed,
and remembers the words that his mother had said:
"When you have a poor day, or your friends treat you bad;
if you have lots of homework, or feel kind of sad;
wherever you are, and whatever you do...
Remember, M.A.D.L.Y. means

'MOM AND DAD LOVE YOU!'"